Tal

THIS SPECIAL SIGNED EDITION IS
LIMITED TO 750 NUMBERED COPIES
AND 26 LETTERED COPIES

THIS IS COPY 425.

Brian Lumley's

FREAKS

Brian Lumley's

FREAKS

Subterranean Press ✱ 2004

Brian Lumley's Freaks

Copyright © Brian Lumley, 2004.
All rights reserved.

Illustrations Copyright © Allen Koslowski, 2004.
All rights reserved.

Interior design Copyright © Tim Holt, 2004.
All rights reserved.

"Foreword" Copyright © Brian Lumley, 2004, appears here for
the first time.

"In the Glow Zone" Copyright © Brian Lumley, 1977, first published in *Cold Fear: New Tales of Terror,* edited by Hugh Lamb.

"Mother Love" Copyright © Brian Lumley, 1971, first published
in *Witchcraft & Sorcery.*

"Problem Child" Copyright © Brian Lumley, 1974, first published in *Vampires, Werewolves and Other Monsters,* edited by
Roger Elwood.

"The Ugly Act" Copyright © Brian Lumley, 1988, first appeared
in *2AM.*

"Somebody Calling" Copyright © Brian Lumley, 2004, appears
here for the first time.

First Edition

ISBN
1-59606-004-2

Subterranean Press
PO Box 190106
Burton, MI 48519

subpress@earthlink.net

www.subterraneanpress.com

Foreword

Freaks? Well, yes, there have been more than one or two such in my work. But face it, what's Horror all about if not freaks and freakishness? I mean, Count Dracula, Frankenstein's Monster and the Wolfman: they aren't exactly normal guys, now are they? And what about all those freaks of nuclear or miscegenetic mutation in the X-Files and the good old Cthulhu Mythos? And even in The Hulk and Swamp Thing, und so weiter, *ad infinitum.* Horror without freaks would be like Westerns without six-shooters, Science Fiction without aliens, Fantasy without dragons, and Porn without pussy.

Myself, I've always had this *thing* for post-nuclear freaks (of the fictional variety as opposed to the Chernobyl kind, you understand) and over the last thirty-five years I've told quite a few stories of this sort…well, four of them at least. And in telling them I've discovered that it's sometimes the shorter stories that pack the hardest punch. Which answers the question of why? in respect of this current, odd little quintet: I simply wanted to group these mordant subgenre items together in order to preserve them in their own jars in the miniature freak-house that you're now holding in your hands.

And speaking of freak-houses, here's a thought for you:

While you might have a laugh at the circus midgets mixing it with the clowns, admire the Tattooed Lady's torso and stare in awe at the Elastic Man's double-jointed contortions, when it comes to the freaks in our favourite genre fictions—well, you wouldn't want to meet up with one of *those* in a dark alley, now would you? (Or on the other hand maybe *you* would, you very sick person you!)

Anyway:

Two of these five tales tell of—and two are told by—weird characters who exist courtesy of post-holocaust radiation and misapplied science, while the fifth is another first-person story told by…by a confused cannibal? (And I accused *you* of being sick!) Only one of the five, "The Ugly Act," required a few stitches here and there before I popped it back in its jar, and while the others have been available for viewing for many

Foreword

years now, "Somebody Calling" is an entirely new exhibit.

So roll up, roll up! 'Cos it's showtime, folks. You pays your money and you takes your chance. The tent's dark entrance beckons, and the freaks are waiting just inside...

Brian Lumley
Torquay, England
December 2003

In the Glow Zone

Mommy is dead.

She is dead and there is no water and no rats left. The water has turned very hard and thick now so we can't fish. And we can't dig roots because the ground is hard too. There was cold-white when we woke up and found Mommy dead. That was three days. She is cold and thin and stiff and still. She is dead. She is like the rats we trap or throw stones at when they are dead. Except they are sometimes fat and she is very thin...

We all cried when we saw her. She had told us she would be dead soon. When the rats were all gone from round here before the water went hard and the cold-white she said it. She told us I am going into town for rats I will be back soon. If I don't come back keep warm. Eat roots and rats and drink river water. Try to find clothes in the villages—*and keep away from men!*

Before she went to town she said this will be the death of me. She meant the Green Glow. Nobody lives in the town, it is all broken down and at night there is the Green Glow. We can see it now fading as the sky gets bright. Mommy is sitting in the corner all stiff and cold. She has a Green Glow too now.

Before she died she said you are to eat me if you get too hungry but please bury my bones and make a little cross to mark the place. We think she did not know what she said. We will not eat her, we would not like that and anyway she has the Green Glow. We never ate rats with the Green Glow and we will not eat Mommy. She once told us the Green Glow is your father, it is more your father than the rotten bastard who ran off on me when the war started. *Men are all bastards* she told us.

When she came back from town we ate. She had small rats and one very big one she called a cat. There were more cats she said but all mutants. This one was a very old cat from before the war. He remembered people and went to her so she could hit him with her axe...The axe is ours now she is dead.

She roasted some rats and we ate but soon she was sick. Next day her hair came out. Next day it came out a lot and blood too. Then she said the Green Glow has got me and I will die.

And she did. And three days are gone and the rats too and the cold-white is here and we are hungry.

Over there is smoke. It has nearly always been there. Mommy only made fires at night. She said she knew the Woman and Her Two who made the fire. She said she had met them long ago when we were little. The Woman was nice but Mommy was frightened of Her Two. They were not sensible they were like animals Mommy said. They aren't like you she said they bite like rats.

The smoke is still there but it is quiet now. Before there was sometimes noise. When there was noise Mommy said they were hunting for food the Woman and Her Two. Then she would make us hide but nobody ever came here...

The Woman and Her Two are very quiet now. Perhaps they are dead like Mommy. We think the *men* got them *men* and their dogs. Dogs are like rats but even bigger than cats Mommy told us. We couldn't see the dogs much but we heard them making loud angry noises. We saw the *men* a lot of them running through the village over there. They had ropes and we saw things jumping on the ropes where the cold-white was deep following the *men*. Because the cold-white is deep we couldn't see the dogs very well but they jumped and made angry noises and we heard them.

We heard the Woman too she was crying very loud and Her Two were making noises like the dogs. That was before dark. In the night the *men* laughed and the Woman made very bad noises. Now there is no noise but the smoke is more than before. We think the *men* made a big fire before they left. The cold-white is falling but over there we still see the smoke.

We know all *men* are bastards because Mommy said so and she said what the bastards would do to us if they found us. We think they did it to the Woman and Her Two. We will only light our fire at night. Then the *men* and their dogs will stay out of the Glow Zone...

Once before when it was warm and there were roots and some fat rats and a few fish a *man* found us. He was a bastard.

When Mommy saw him coming she said hide and we did. He didn't see us right off but we could see him. He didn't say a lot but we knew Mommy was frightened she was frightened of the *man*. We never saw a *man* before he was a lot like Mommy. He had a stick-thing. Mommy gave him some fish to eat and showed him a place to sleep when he was asleep she came to us and said he might be OK you stay there and when he wakes up he might go away. *Don't let him see you* she said. She said he has a gun it is that stick-thing he carries it can kill very quick.

While she was talking the *man* got up and came over. He said what you got there in the back and shoved Mommy out of the way. Then he said Goddamn might have known it a girl like you alone in the Glow Zone well you treat me right and there'll be no trouble.

He caught hold of Mommy's hair and started to pull her and we moved at him. He looked very frightened he pointed the stick-thing Mommy said *no stay where you are it's all right.* We knew it wasn't...

It got dark soon we stayed where we were and listened to the funny noises in the dark. The *man* was making a lot of little noises and Mommy was crying but quietly. It was very dark when she came to us she said go get the axe the bastard's really asleep this time we'll kill him but let me get his gun first.

We got the axe she got his gun and he came awake. Mommy stood back and we got hold of him quick before he could stand and hit him in the body with the axe. *No no* Mommy said *his head get his head.* He was shouting *oh my god my god* we hit him in the head. There was a lot of blood.

Next morning Mommy said we won't bury such as him he'll feed the fish so we took him to the river. His body moved slow in the water towards town right in the middle of the Glow Zone. Serve the bastard right Mommy said.

It is very cold we think of a fire. A fire will bring *men* but not if we use the Woman and Her Two's fire. We think they must be dead. Anyway we are cold.

We go to where the smoke rises through the cold-white. Nearly there we find things we think they must be the Woman's Two. They are dead and stiff there is a lot of blood and little holes in them. We see how they look and remember what Mommy said we are glad they are dead. The Woman is near the fire she has no clothes she is stiff and cold. There is blood on her face and body she looks a lot like Mommy and we are sad. She is dead. There is a cave in a big heap of bricks it has a blanket hanging at the front. The Woman and Her Two lived there we think. We move towards the cave perhaps it is warm.

There is a loud dog noise a dog jumps at us through the cold-white. We grab him and hit with the axe he is dead. A *man* comes through the blanket in front of the cave he says *what the hell.*

Jesus Christ boys lookee here he points his stick-thing called a gun and we rush at him. We are angry all *men* are bastards. There is a very loud noise and we are hurt. We are hit in our body and the gun has smoke but we don't stop running on all our hands and legs. The *man* points his gun again but we are on him. We knock down the gun we swing our axe at his head. There is blood on the cold-white the *man* is down we stamp on him.

The blanket is torn down other *men* the *men* from last night are there they have guns. All the guns are making loud noises and we are hurt very bad in the body. One man turns to run when we

are near and we hit him hard our axe sticks in his back when he falls he makes loud noises.

One other bastard says *great god in…will you look at what a bloody—look out!* We rush at him but the guns are loud and there is much blood from our body and too much hurt. We jump on the *man* and pull an arm off him and stomp on him.

Now there are dogs jumping and they have teeth. We are torn the guns hurt we fall down in the cold-white it is red now.

One of our heads is hit we hurt so much we crash all our arms and legs.

Our body is all red we are very tired.

Another head is hit.

Another…We will soon be dead our body will be stiff and cold.

Like Mommy.

Problem Child

My symptoms, Dr. Trent said, were those of developing schizophrenia, split personality, but I could "counter such tendencies by recording details of them diary-wise, or by talking to yourself about them, thus recognizing and resolving the peculiarities of your dualism when controlled by your more 'normal' archetype." Ye Gods! Do they *all* talk like that, I wonder? Still, he sounded like he knew what he was talking about, and so—

Since my hands weren't much for writing, I started to talk to myself. And you know, his idea was all right in a way; that is, chatting to myself about it did seem to help—initially. But now, well, I don't see old Trent anymore, I haven't for a long, long time.

Wonder how he's getting on. Trent the quack—the so-called "psychiatrist"—the head-shrinker. I should never have taken my problem to him in the first place.

My "problem!"

I suspect that old Trent was laughing at me really, that he never did believe me. Even then, though, I could have proved the things I told him...if I had really wanted to. I could have cut my nails for him—and then stayed around while they grew again!

"Six times a day?" I remember him asking. "You cut your nails *six times a day?* Well, they look perfectly normal nails to me!"

And it was true, they were perfectly normal nails—to look at! But they simply grew too fast. They still do; in fact the speed at which they grow has increased! Until recently I was cutting them up to eight times daily. Now I just don't bother. And I remember how, if I slept for more than three hours at a stretch...

It's murder to wake up and find your nails long and black and—hooked!

And I used to worry about getting jackets to fit my hump; but knowing what I know now—well, who needs jackets?

My hump: I remember when I was a kid, just a little kid, how my friends used to say I had a small hump. Now I have a big hump. I once went for treatment for curvature of the spine...Hah!

Problem Child

There's a laugh. "Curvature of the spine," indeed! It made life hell at the orphanage, though.

Of course in those days I didn't have my fingernail-toenail thing. That didn't start until I was out of my teens, till after I left the orphanage, and even then the growth rate wasn't much in the beginning. Like the hair. I remember when I first started to shave my chin. What's more, I remember when I started shaving my body!

You should try to imagine the difficulty living when you can't go out in public for more than two or three hours at a stretch. Life was *not* easy. In the end I got a job as a nightwatchman…

By then I had given up shaving my chest, arms, and legs; I simply concentrated on my face. This was so that I could sit by my nightwatchman's brazier in those hours when the last drunks are going home without attracting too much attention. In the quieter hours of the night I would shave again, as often as I needed it, and I'd also cut my nails, which had been bothering me for some time by then.

It's really surprising how many nightwatchmen have humps…

I lived in a boardinghouse. A sleazy place moldering on the outskirts of the city. I had a room on the ground floor, and I could sneak out unnoticed when I wanted to. Not that that was very often; rarely during daylight. It was all too much. All that shaving and cutting…and creaming.

Creaming! Have I mentioned my skin? No, I haven't mentioned my skin. Well, that didn't begin until after all my other little blemishes were well established. My skin started to rough over.

Rough over?—regular ichthyosis, it was—like psoriasis gone rampant, with knobs on! I had to cream the skin on my face before I could do anything or go anywhere. I used a skin-colored cream, a "woman's preparation," which did the job pretty well. Makes you wonder, though, what lurks beneath the surface of some of those dolly faces in the girlie magazines, doesn't it?

Of course, in the early days, I saw a doctor about it (a *real* doctor, as opposed to old Trent) but he could do nothing—except fill useless prescriptions. After a few visits he wouldn't even see me. I don't think he liked my bad breath.

The whole thing reached a head some six months back when I started to go off my food. Up until then I could fancy almost anything—eggs, fish, beans—anything I could cook up for myself or get out of a can. It started when I got sick every time I ate something. Soon it had reached the stage where I would open a can and gag at the very smell of the contents, no matter what. I remember leaving a can of chopped steak lying around open and untouched for over a week. I was living on bread and water by then, but even so I was still sick sometimes. On the ninth day I ate the steak straight out of the can. I wasn't sick! I ate stinking, rotten steak for a long time before it dawned on me to come and live here. By then it had also dawned on me what was "wrong" with me.

It's simply this: there's *nothing* wrong with me!

I mean, just think about it: hands spade-shaped and hard as hell, for digging; a mouth (have I mentioned my mouth?) like a sucker, for slurping up soft stuff; big square teeth—I've *always* had them—for grinding hard stuff; flaky, blotched skin and black tufts of coarse hair all over my body, matching up perfectly with the shadows and mottled background of my natural habitat...

Yes, *natural*—for me!

I remember (it seems like years ago) a record by someone who used to sing Country and Western songs. It was about a boy named Sue, and how that boy hunted down his father for giving him a girl's name. I, too, will hunt down my father. One night I'll leave this place and hunt him down. I'll find him, and there and then I'll kill him with my claw hands and suck him up with my sucker mouth, and grind him with my strong, square teeth.

My mother, too.

Oh, they didn't call me Sue. They didn't call me anything, just left me on the doorstep of the orphanage. Was I so—abnormal? Did I look so—freakish? They could have hid me, brought me along until I fitted in with them. Or perhaps there were others with them who wouldn't allow it, who feared that my presence (I imagine I made a pretty human-looking baby) might attract the attention of…people.

They couldn't afford that, I suppose. After all, it's only recently, so to speak, that people have stopped believing in *my* kind. My race has all but died out in the minds of men; like fairies and vampires and werewolves—but *I* know we're real!

Yes, one night I'll go away from here and make my way in the shadows to another place. It'll need to be soon for there's no food here now. Perhaps I'll pick up a couple of the nightwatchmen on the way! And when we've cleaned the next place out, then we'll move on again. And one night I'll find my father.

Oh!—I'll find him, all right. One night. Sooner or later. I'll find him…

After all, there aren't that many graveyards…

The Ugly Act

No one should be born as ugly as Hesch Blarzt; so ugly that at first sight they believed the placenta hadn't bothered to wait its turn. And certainly no one that ugly should also be unlucky enough to live. Indeed if Hesch had been born just a couple of decades later he wouldn't have been allowed to live, but in 2129 the Ugly Act hadn't yet been introduced.

The Ugly Act, as its either beautiful or extremely rich proponents could have told you, was designed to get Old Mother Earth all nice and green and tidy and unpolluted again—which meant doing away with anything that was likely to clutter the planet up or make it look unpretty. Like, for instance, Hesch Blarzt.

2147 was the year of the Ugly Act—which forced the big industrial combines to bury their trash under forests of giant GM ferns that grew and sucked out all the rubbish and turned it into purple tendrils and huge smelly red flowers, leaving nothing but a soft gray ash behind that made a damn good fertilizer—but at the time of which I write all of that was still eighteen years away, and that was when Hesch Blarzt was born.

His parents took one look at him, denied all responsibility, put Hesch in a home and ran off to the moon to grow low-grav tomatoes. Five years later the moon got atmosphere and the Blarzts looked like living happily ever after...except Hesch.

Of course, if people had looked close enough they would have seen that he was a mutant, the result of three generations of Blarzts working in experimental hydroponics, which involved a degree of proximity to certain industrial radioactives. His was a classic case of jelled genes.... But nobody looked that close. Few could even bear to.

By the time Hesch was twenty-one and ready to be kicked out of the orphanage where he'd been trained to fuel furnaces (which particular work would keep him more or less out of sight in the bowels of the city, tending to the central heating), the Ugly Act was three years old. Moon tomatoes had fallen through when people discovered they could eat giant flowering ferns, but Hesch's folks had got out of moon farming early

and were doing great in Darkside nickel-iron and uranium.

And so, down in the sweaty, dirty, dark environment of the city's basest basement, Hesch grew to manhood...which, being a slow starter and all, took him another three years.

Naturally—what with all the murders, muggings, riots, gang-bangs and what have you—few self-respecting young women would dream of going out at night in the city; they only very rarely went out in daylight! And that left Hesch in kind of a hole. For he was beginning to feel the sap rise (in fact it had been rising for years, which accounted for his many pimples), and no satisfactory way to tap the sap.

He'd tried the whorehouses, certainly, but the androids were too mechanical, and real live whores were too expensive. Also, where the latter were concerned...well, Hesch wasn't growing any prettier. The only live one he ever had, he'd had to pour a half-bottle of fern wine down her neck before she'd even look at him, and even then she'd made him wear a handsome mask first.

You see, Hesch wasn't just ugly. He was *ugly!* In the mid-twentieth century he would probably have gotten along okay; lots of people were very unlovely in those days. But since then, why, man and womankind just kept getting prettier. So anyone who was seventy-seven inches tall, awkward with it, large-pored, hook-nosed, bow-legged, coarse-haired, *and* warty to boot simply didn't stand a chance in AD 2153. The people at the home had done Hesch a real favour putting him in furnace-stoking: there were campaigners "up top" (meaning on the surface levels) who were all for extending the Ugly Act to include anyone below a Grade Three Pretty—which wasn't far short of devastatingly beautiful!

The world was kind of crowded—even the moon was getting that way—and natural disasters and small-country wars just weren't doing their bit to keep the numbers down. For the last couple of years the population explosion had been more a nova. Of course, most of these people who wanted a law passed to put something like thiry-six percent of the world's population down were all very rich; rich enough that if they weren't beautiful already, they could become beautiful very, very quickly.

Plastic surgeons were rich, too, and getting richer every day as the Ugly Act tightened its grip. And yet they were still poor compared with some. Anybody who owned a quarter acre, for instance, was a multimillionaire in an age when you could walk houseboat decks from Long Island to New Haven. And so, since men were having trouble settling the planets—and since flowering fern and quahog chowder didn't taste half so good as sweet and sour pork—naturally the withits were looking for a way to do away with the withouts, and the Pretties wanted rid of all the Unpretties…and

The Ugly Act

Hesch Blarzt fitted both unwanted categories perfectly.

Saturday afternoons and Sundays, when he wasn't working, Hesch would put on a handsome mask and walk the lower levels of the city. His size kept the muggers away. Now and then he would catch a glimpse of a girl, usually as she turned to run. They'd run if anyone looked at them twice, what with all the crime and what have you; but someone as tall as Hesch, who also *shuffled*...that was just too much. Now and then some overzealous cop would stop him and whip out a gun, ram the barrel up one of his large nostrils under his handsome mask and yell, "Hey, you, Grot! You never heard of the Ugly Act?"

Of course, the Ugly Act didn't apply to Hesch— not just yet, but it was very worrying anyway. Pretty soon now...well, he reckoned he had about a year left, two at the outside.

And it was probably this sort of anxiety that brought to light the other side of Hesch's mutation: his ability to zoop. It happened this way:

He was sitting in his little cell (his so-called flatlet; but since furnace stokers didn't rate very high in the social order, it was the size of a small cell) watching this obscene minitele show one night, when suddenly a startling, incredibly silly thought occurred to him: how it would be quite splendid to own an uninhabited island. And later, lying in his bunk in the darkness, the thought returned; he saw a detailed picture of the island in his mind's eye. And it was very beautiful.

Now, uninhabited islands were nonexistent. Every habitable piece of real estate on the entire planet was simply crawling with people, so obviously Hesch's little bit of escapism was simply, well, escapism. Except he'd been wishing very determinedly, and—*zoop!*

Just like that, the darkness of his cell turned to bright sunlight on the golden sands of a wonderful uninhabited island! An island with palm trees and a fresh, clear stream bubbling down from a central hill and a sky bluer than Hesch had ever dreamed of, without a trace of smog. And no people, not a one, except Hesch. Which soon proved to be the one big drawback.

Night came on and the stars came out, amazingly bright in the smokeless atmosphere, and Hesch lay on his back on the hill beside the little stream, and there was no Ugly Act and everything was very wonderful. Except that he was lonely…

*

In the morning Hesch had a coconut for breakfast then went for a swim. The water was cool but not cold; fairly large fish swam in small schools; there wasn't the slightest hint of a current or even a tide. It could have been the Mediterranean a couple of hundred years ago, but he knew it

wasn't. An island such as this couldn't possibly have escaped humanity's explosion; and beside that, the stars hadn't been right when he'd gazed up at them in the night. No, this place Hesch had zooped off to was other than mundane.

He spent three days there, living on fish, nuts, fresh clean water like none tasted on Earth since immediately after the last ice age, then zooped back to his cell. There he sat and thought about it for a while, then put on a handsome mask and went for a walk in the city. He got a lot of funny looks, saw perhaps half a million people in half an hour—of which total maybe fifty were women—was threatened three times by policemen, then returned to his flatlet.

Four hundred and ninety-nine thousand, nine hundred and fifty men were forgotten as soon as the door closed behind him and he was alone— but not the fifty women. And not the three policemen...

It was getting bad and Hesch knew it. It seemed the only thing people were talking about was the Ugly Act, to which he would surely become subject and soon. If only there was a woman on his island. She didn't have to be a Grade One Pretty, (hell, could he afford to be choosy?) Just as long as she—

But what was he *thinking* about? If he could zoop himself, mightn't he be able to zoop someone else? Like maybe the prettiest goddam Pretty in the city?

Taking an elevator up sixteen levels, Hesch went out again onto the city's evening streets. But even as he left the elevator a policeman grabbed his right arm, bending it up behind his back. "Are you Hesch Blarzt?" the cop asked, making it a statement of fact.

"I am he," Hesch answered in his deep, croaking voice. "Is something wrong?"

"Yeah. You stopped working."

"Is that a crime?"

"Yeah. Everybody contributes, Grot. We've all got to keep working as efficiently as possible to help the ecology, to help Nature balance it all out, and to comply with the Ugly Act."

"You are brainwashed, fellow," answered Hesch. "Man ruined his environment decades ago. The world is dying; it is poisoned and recycling its own poisons. All the Ugly Act will do is slow it down some, but never enough. The corpse will only support so many maggots before it falls apart, and soon we'll have to move on. And by the way, you are hurting my arm."

"Hey, you're not only really grot, Grot," said the cop, "you're also stupid! I don't know if anyone ever told you, but really ugly buggers like you aren't supposed to mouth off. Did you know that? What happened anyway—you forgot your handsome mask or something?"

He twisted Hesch's arm very hard and smiled up at him with white teeth that flashed in his young, naturally handsome face. It was almost angelic, that face. Hesch couldn't understand why a crud like this deserved a face like that.

"I did forget my mask, sir, yes," he answered, pain twisting his features into even less lovable lines. "Do you—*uh!*—swim?"

"Swim?" Such an abrupt change in the mood and direction of the conversation took the cop by surprise. "What are you trying to accuse me of? They're making pools illegal, even you should know that. There's no excuse for waste of that magnitude. What, water to *swim* in? Water's for drinking, Grot."

"I learned to swim at the orphanage, in a static—*uh!*—water tank."

"So what?"

"So that gives me the—*uh!*—advantage."

"Yeah? You think there'll be a deluge before I can get you to the station?" The cop opened his mouth to laugh, and several pints of salt water rushed into it. Hesch had zooped the two of them onto his island. Well, he'd zooped himself onto it, at any rate. The cop he'd zooped into the sea.

Hesch stood on the golden beach massaging his arm and dispassionately watching the black-uniformed man drowning. Then, in a moment of remorse, he quickly zooped the cop back to his own world. Alone again, he stared at the concentric ripples on the surface of an otherwise still ocean, and grinned hideously—which was the only possible way someone with his looks could grin. He could imagine the scene as a thoroughly soaked, half-drowned cop suddenly arrived out of nowhere into the crowded evening city.

Then the grin slipped from his face as he realized that he didn't have too much time now. Next time, he'd probably be shot on sight. And holding that thought he zooped back to his little cell and put on his handsome mask.

He took a different elevator to a recreation level. In one of the halls a frenzied crowd was watching a bleedie, relieving their pent up hatreds, anxieties, and frustrations by screaming obscenities at the 3D stage. One act showed an ugly man, almost as ugly as Hesch, throwing himself into a steam-driven blender. It was all very explicit, and the mob went wild when grey, simulated brain matter and purple-veined entrails rained down on them from concealed ducts in the ceiling.

Looking up, Hesch spotted a couple in a private box. The woman was very beautiful. Hesch zooped her onto his island and approached her from a safe distance along the beach. She saw him coming and put a trembling hand up to her mouth.

"'Lo," said Hesch. "This is my island."

"How…how did I get here?" Her voice trembled.

Hesch offered a shrug (why should he go into details?) and croaked, "There's plenty to eat here—and I can teach you how to swim."

The Ugly Act

Something of the horror of this impossible thing that was happening to her sank in, and with a little shriek she fainted. Hesch carried her into the cool shade of a palm, where he propped her with her head against the rough bole. Then he prepared a coconut, caught some fish, built a fire and sat back waiting for her to wake up.

When she came to he had a line already worked out.

He didn't know how they came to be on the island, he told her, but they were in the same boat together. They would simply have to make the best of it. He was a man, she was a woman...there was plenty to eat, and he would teach her how to swim.

When she started to cry he put on his handsome mask and went for a shambling walk along the beach. An hour later when he came back she was still sobbing her heart out. She hadn't touched the coconut and the fish were black and smoking where they hung over the fire.

She looked up at him through her tears and said, "You did this to me, didn't you? You brought me here for...something. How *could* you?" She was a nice young woman, and suddenly Hesch felt ugly and unclean. He was used to feeling ugly but the uncleanliness was something new.

"Uh—sorry!" he said, and zooped her right back to the city. Then, after a short period of dejection and a shorter one of considered thought, Hesch had an idea. Zooping himself into a whorehouse he asked for a live one. The madame sniffed doubtfully, but took Hesch's money anyway—his total life-savings, maybe enough to buy synthetic groceries for one for a month—then gave him the key to an upstairs nest.

As he climbed the stairs, Hesch told himself it made no difference: a woman was a woman was a woman. At least a prostitute shouldn't be too awkward about...things. After all, he had a whole lot to offer, really.

He let himself into the nest and closed the door. Behind a curtain of beads a figure stirred languorously. The light was only poor, so that when she parted the beads she couldn't quite see him at first. "Hey! A really *big* boy!" she cooed, then got close up. "Ow!" she exclaimed then, drawing back. And: "What a *Grot!*"

"I own a whole island," said Hesch, "and—"

"Out, you ugly bugger!" she told him. "There are certain things even I don't do. And you're one of them."

"Listen," said Hesch, "I am quite desperate, and I really do have a very lovely—"

"*Out!*" she yelled.

So Hesch zooped her onto his island, which he'd intended doing from the start. It stood to reason she'd be more amenable to persuasion there. "This is my island," he told her, as she sat down abruptly in the golden sand and stared in amazement at the sea, the sky, the waving palm trees.

The Ugly Act

"Your island," she repeated him faintly.

"Yes, and there's plenty of fresh food here. And, er, if you would like to learn to swim, I—"

"Swim?" She jumped to her feet and attacked him furiously, slapping his face while he put up his hands to protect himself. "I don't want to fucking swim! I want to go back home!"

"Home?" Hesch held her off and shook his head sadly. "To the whorehouse? How long do you think that will last? The Ugly Act will soon do away with the brothels—the common or garden sort, at least—and you'll all be outlawed, removed, erased. Prostitution is ugly."

"So are the bleedies," she came back, "but they're doing well enough."

"The bleedies are a diversion," said Hesch, "designed to take the public's mind off the Ugly Act on the one hand, while preparing for it on the other. Believe me, the end is nigh for the bleedies, too. And that time is coming fast!"

She was looking more closely at the island now, big-eyed and curious, thinking to herself that Hesch was probably right. She saw the huge ripe nuts on the palms, fish jumping in the sea, the sparkling stream. She felt the sun warm on her skin, not hidden away behind poisonous clouds, and felt strangely caressed by the warm breeze that oh-so-gently moved the palm fronds.

"You *own* this place?" she finally said. "I mean, you? So where is everybody?"

"There's no one else here. Just we two," Hesch answered, moving closer.

She took another look at the island and decided that she liked it. In fact, there seemed to be only one thing wrong with it. Long ago she'd had her fill of men, but a girl has to eat. Here, however, she could eat without men. And she could definitely eat without Hesch Blarzt. Indeed, his absence would be a positive incentive to eating; without a doubt it would help in keeping the food down.

She reached up and put one arm around Hesch's neck, but as he bent to encircle her waist she drew out a long straight pin from concealment in her belt. Out the corner of his eye, at the last moment, Hesch saw silver flash in the sun as she aimed the deadly pin at his side. He zooped her away as hard as he could, without direction, and heard her rapidly diminishing scream, an echo that vanished into emptiness. She hadn't gone back to the whorehouse, nor anywhere on Earth, Hesch was aware of that. He wasn't exactly sure *where* she'd gone, and he didn't much care. She hadn't been worthy of his plan after all, and he was angry with himself that he'd ever believed such a thing might work.

Then he heard something; something so unexpected that at first he failed to recognize the sound. It was a splashing from along the golden sands. Someone was bathing in the sea, singing in a low, cracked—female?—voice. Hesch squinted

his little eyes and looked along the beach. A sun-browned figure splashed noisily at the edge of the ocean. Hesch moved warily along the beach wondering how this could possibly have happened.

He knew that he hadn't zooped this unknown woman onto his island, so who had? Or maybe this was only one island of many; maybe this was an entire world, populated but thinly, and maybe this woman was only visiting the island. He at once looked for a boat but couldn't see one.

He felt a little disappointed on the one hand, excited on the other. If this was some other world he'd zooped himself onto, and not a parallel dimension as he'd suspected...well, it seemed most unlikely that the inhabitants of a planet like this would have an Ugly Act. And if there was no Ugly Act, and nothing but a handful of friendly, happy people, why—

"How did you get onto my island?" she asked in fractured, grunting tones, staring at him squint-eyed from the blue sea.

Hesch was astonished. "Your island?" he said. "But this is *my* island."

"Oh, really? Is that so?" Her voice took on a definitely amused if somewhat gravelly tone. "And just how did you get to be the owner?"

"Why I...I just zooped here! It's a thing I do, a means of getting about, and I—"

"And since no one was here, you took it upon yourself to assume ownership," she finished for him.

"Er, yes."

"Turn your back, I'm coming out," she said.

Hesch turned his back and she left the water and shrugged into a worn dress. "Okay," she told him. "You can turn around now."

Hesch did so and looked at her. And in a little while he said, "I think I get it now. You zooped here too, just like me, to escape the Ugly Act."

"Right," she answered.

He studied her more closely. Apart from her squinting eyes which were dissimilarly coloured— her hair was tangled, her shoulders sagged, and her legs were too short. She was a mess. And yet, strangely, there was a kind of kindness about her.

"Well," he said, "since we're both strangers in a strange, empty land, I guess that makes us joint owners."

She shook her head. "No, *I* own this island."

"And what gives *you* the right of ownership?"

"I made the island," she said, grinning lopsid-edly.

"Oh, come now—" Hesch began, but stopped short when he found himself floundering in the sea. The island had shrunk to a cartoon-sized beach with a single palm tree. She sat beneath the tree while he swam slowly back and forth.

"I made it," she said again, "and I can unmake it whenever I want to. If I fancied I could just zoop off elsewhere, taking my island with me and leaving you right here."

"I would zoop back to Earth," Hesch countered her threat, but still felt slightly alarmed.

"Back to the Ugly Act?" She cocked her head on one side.

"I could maybe find some other island to zoop to...some other planet even."

"There are no other islands," she said. "I didn't make any others. As for other planets...you want to try? I've tried it already. There are worlds you'd freeze to death on in a matter of minutes, and others that will fry you black in half as long. There are planets where the atmosphere is so poisonous your insides would melt in as much time as it takes to tell, and where acid rain falls on semi-molten continents. But as shitty as it is, there's no place like Earth."

"There's this place."

"Yes, but I made it. It's a place in my head, and it will only exist as long as I exist."

"Perhaps," Hesch considered aloud, swimming to and fro in the crystal sea, "perhaps I can also, er, make an island."

"Go ahead and try it," she answered. "I wish you the best of luck. For it must be obvious that there's no room for you on my island."

"Don't concern yourself," grated Hesch. "I wasn't planning on staying—not with you here. You remind me too much of the Ugly Act."

"Now you're being deliberately cruel," she said, enlarging the island until Hesch stood on dry land, dripping salt water. "Perhaps it'll help you concentrate if you don't have to swim."

"Concentrate?"

"You need all the concentration you can muster in order to make an island."

So Hesch concentrated as hard as he could, but no island. "No good," he finally admitted defeat. Then he brightened. "So maybe I can get you to make one for me?"

"No chance." She shook her head. "It's enough of a problem keeping this place going. Two islands would be twice as hard."

"Well, all right," said Hesch reluctantly. "I...I guess I'll be going, then."

She nodded, but he made no attempt to go. And she seemed equally uncertain about making a move. So for a long time they simply looked at each other. And it was a funny thing, but the longer they looked the less ugly each appeared to the other.

"What do you intend doing, er, when I've gone?" he asked her.

She blushed furiously, which strangely enough improved her looks—well, a little. But Hesch only noticed her confusion.

"I...I...well, I—" she stuttered and stumbled.

And Hesch cried, "Well I'll be damned! So that's it, eh?"

"What is what?" she asked, reddening more yet.

"They didn't want you, did they?"

"Who?" she asked. "What are you talking about?"

"All the men you've zooped to the island," Hesch answered. "All of the Pretties you've brought here. Everything you had to offer, still they didn't want you. Hah! The same thing happened to me."

She began to cry. "All of my life," she sniffled brokenly, "I have dreamed of a handsome prince of a man who would love me like none other; and yes, I've brought men to this island, only to discover that—"

"I know," Hesch interrupted, nodding sadly.

"They called me names," she went on, "and—"

"Names like 'Grot,' and 'Freak,' and—"

"All of those things." She nodded. "Yes."

He sighed and said, "My experience was precisely the same. For all that the Earth is polluted and rotten, and yes, ugly—far more ugly than you or I—they prefer it. And I've come to understand why."

"Oh?" She looked at him.

"Maggots," he explained, "much prefer dead meat to fresh. And they also prefer the company of their own kind. The Earth is dead, where people have become like maggots swarming in her dead flesh. But this place, your island, is *alive!*"

"Do you really like my island, Mr., er—?"

"Hesch," he told her. "Hesch Blarzt. Yes, indeed I do like it."

"Then please stay a little longer if you wish. But be gone when I get back."

"You intend to try again then, Miss, er—?"

"Gyff," she answered. "Miss Gyffarl Twell. Gyff for short. And yes, I'll try one more time."

"I shall be gone," Hesch said, "when you return, Gyff."

With which she zooped.

*

And so, fully intending to take his departure...soon, Hesch wandered along the beach and rolled up his trousers to splash his legs in the water. He climbed the hill to watch the clean spring water cascade over washed pebbles gleaming like jewels in the sun. He felt the gentle breeze on his skin and watched the changing pattern of dappled light under the fronds of the sighing palms. And though he hadn't intended it, still he was there when Gyff got back with a man— a young policeman with an angelic face that Hesch recognized immediately!

Hesch hid behind a thick-boled palm and watched. The cop had at first fallen on his behind in the sand, shock draining his face, but in another second he jumped to his feet. "You," he snarled, grabbing Gyff by the hair. "You must be in league with *him!* And I'll bet you terrorists have got something to do with the blowup, too!"

"In league with whom?" she cried, trying to free herself.

"With that Grot who damn near drowned me!" he yelled at her, snatching out his gun and striking her across the side of the head. Too dazed to do anything, Gyff crumpled to the sand. "I don't know just exactly how you two shits do it," the young, handsome cop rasped, "but I'll damn well soon find out!"

With his free fist buried deep in her hair, he hauled Gyff to her feet and made to strike her again—at which Hesch came out from under the palm and shouted, "Here I am, you fiend!"

Hesch might simply have zooped the brute back to Earth, but he wanted Gyff to see how things really were—wanted her to realize, as he now realized, that the gulf between was truly impassable. As the cop heard Hesch's gravelly voice he released Gyff, turned and fired all in one smooth movement. Hesch zooped just in time.

"Here I am," he called again, from farther down the beach. Again the cop whirled, fired off a second shot, and again Hesch zooped. "Here I am—"

But this time, as the black-clad Pretty lined Hesch up in his sights, Gyff gave a little shriek and cried, "No! No more! You...*go!*" And she pointed at the cop.

He went, leaving an echo, a scream that quickly dwindled into emptiness. *Well,* Hesch told himself, *at least the prostitute's no longer alone—wherever she is!*

"That was horrible, *horrible!*" cried Gyff, as Hesch went to her. Throwing herself into his arms, she said, "It was like…like a bleedie!"

"You mean to say you fancied *him?*" Hesch's voice, for all that it grated, somehow managed to signal his disbelief.

"No," she shook her head. "Oh no, never—but he grabbed me while I was running in the city, and—"

"Running?"

"Yes. Oh, Hesch, you can't go back there. You must promise to stay here. The moon has exploded and the world's gone mad!"

"What? The moon, exploded? But how?"

"It must have been an accident," she answered. "It started at the refinery on Darkside, then became a chain reaction. Bits of the moon are flying through space like so much shrapnel, and the tides have gone insane. Polluted tsunami are drowning every coastal town and city in poisoned water, and it seems the whole world is destroying itself…"

"The rotten apple falls from the tree," mused Hesch.

"Hesch," she said, her sigh like broken bottles, "you are so…so good. Won't you stay here with me?"

Hesch opened his mouth, closed it, shrugged, and finally said, "Er, yes. I guess so."

"Maybe one day," she said, after a little while, "we'll be able to go back."

"I don't think I'll ever want to," he told her. "Maybe we won't need to go back. If the children inherit your ability to make islands, then—"

"Children?" She drew back a pace and squinted up at him.

"Children, sure," he said, and shrugged. "Why not?"

And when the stars came out, then, warmed by a small fire, they indulged in their own private ugly act. Except it was perfectly beautiful. For after all, beauty lies in the eyes of the beholder...

Mother Love

With a high-pitched whine the bullet took a long groove out of the rock wall to his right, showering him with sharp splinters. He flung himself awkwardly to the ground, feeling a splash of blood on his face where one of the hot, flying fragments had caught him. Simultaneous with the second crack of the rifle, another bullet kicked up dirt in his eyes with a buzz and a thud as it buried itself in the ground a few inches in front of his nose. He waited for a few seconds, blood pounding, before peering cautiously from his prone position along the narrow rock passage to where the girl stood—tattered denims molding the fine shape of her wide-spread legs—squinting down the sights of her weapon...sights which centered squarely on him!

"Lady, if you're planning to scare me, you've done it already. If you're trying to kill me, aim a little more carefully—I hate the thought of bleeding to death…" His voice carried to her, a hoarse, panting shout as she began to squeeze the trigger for the third shot. She eased her finger slowly out of the triggerguard to leave it lying there, a thought's distance from sudden death.

"What are you after?" The way she said it— menacing, low so he could hardly hear—it was more than a question; it was a warning, and he knew he would have to answer carefully. Only sixty feet separated them and there was nowhere he could run. If she was any good at all with that rifle she could put a neat hole right through his head before he made five yards.

"Lady, I seen your fire-smoke earlier in the day, and I smelled your cooking a mile off. Smelled pretty good to a man who hasn't ate in three days—and when I did last eat it was a rat I was lucky enough to catch!" His panting came a little easier now. "But lady, if you want me to move on…you just say the word and I'll be on my way. I'd be plenty obliged, though, if you'd allow me a bite to eat first."

"Get up," she ordered. As he climbed to his feet she stared at the stump where his right arm should have been. "You can't be a mutant—you're too old for that."

He walked slowly, carefully up the defile, dusting himself off as he went towards the girl who was outlined, now, against the evening greens and browns of the small valley behind her. She had a nice set-up here, and she was alone—otherwise she wouldn't be toting that rifle herself. As he drew closer to her he saw the cave on the other side of the valley. Could hardly be more than a hundred yards across, that valley; more a saddle between the hills. Corn patch growing nicely…mutant strawberries…rabbits. She had real good legs…

She saw right where he was looking.

"Hold it right there." He came to a halt not ten feet away from her. "I asked you a question!" She swung the rifle to point it significantly at his middle.

"Mutant? No, industrial accident, that's all—long before the war," he answered. "But I've been given the mutant treatment ever since. So has every cripple! Been kicked out of every town I ever went near for almost four years. It's no fun, lady—'specially now they're burning mutants! Look, if you've any decency at all, you'll give me just a bite of what you've got cooking over there, and then I'll be on my way."

She thought about it, began to shake her head negatively, then changed her mind: "You're… welcome—but I'll warn you now, there's three unmarked graves in the corner of this valley. You try anything…I'll have no more corners left." She waved him past with the gun, taking a good look at him as he went. He was about thirty-five, forty perhaps. He'd probably put on age fast after the war. Feeling her eyes on his stump, he glanced back over his shoulder.

"Armless, I be," he said in wry humour, gratified to see her relax a little. Then: "How come you're up here on your own? You've been here some years by the look of the place."

"I lived in the town on the coast back there, where the walls shine at night," she gestured vaguely behind her. "That place at the foot of the hills, just a heap of rubble now, you must have come through it to get up here. I was only eighteen then…when the war came. One of the first bombs landed in the sea, threw radioactive water all over the town. When my baby was born he was— different. The radiation…" She faltered, lost for words. "…My husband died quickly. What few people lived through it wanted to have my baby put…they wanted to kill him. Said it would be better for him. Said it would be better for both of us. I ran off. I stole the rifle, shells, some seeds and one or two other odds and ends. Been here ever since. I get along fine…"

"You still got the mu—?" He knew it was a mistake before the words were out. The air seemed to go hard.

"Mister," she poked the barrel of the gun viciously between his shoulder blades, "if you're a mutant hunter you're as good as dead!" He staggered from the pressure of the rifle in his back, turning to face her, going suddenly white as he saw her finger tightening on the trigger.

"No...! No, just curious. Christ, I've been hunted myself—and it's obvious I couldn't be a mutant! What, me? A mutant hunter! Why?—some places there's a bounty, sure—but out here in the middle of nowhere? I mean...do I look like a bounty hunter...?" He was pathetic.

She relaxed again. "My baby...he...he died! No more questions." It was an order.

They had crossed the valley and the sun was starting to sink behind the hills. He peered eagerly into the pot hanging over the fire. The cave was a dark blot behind the glowing embers, with a homemade candle flickering at its back.

This was sure a good thing she'd got, he mused to himself, licking his lips.

She motioned with the rifle, indicating he should help himself from the pot. He took up a battered tin plate and heaped it with the thick, bubbling stew before dropping the heavy iron spoon back into the pot. Juicy rabbit bones protruded from the meat in the mess of stew on his plate. Without another word he started eating. It was good.

As he ate he looked the girl over. She had a good face to match her figure. He could hardly keep from staring at the way her shirt swelled outwards with the pressure of the firm breasts beneath it. And it was that above all else—the way her shirt strained from her body—which finally decided his course of action.

He licked his lips and reached casually for the spoon again, crouching with the plate on his knees...

In a second he had straightened and the hot stuff was on her neck. Before she even had time to yelp from the shock he had brought her a savage, whiplash, backhand blow across the face with the swing of a powerfully muscled left arm. As she spun sideways he nimbly grabbed the falling rifle out of midair and turned it on her. She started to scramble to her feet, a red welt already blossoming on her face.

"Stay put!" He held the rifle loosely in his hand, confident finger on the trigger, daring her to make a false move. "I'll shoot you in the legs," he said, grinning wolfishly, "so's not to spoil you completely. You wouldn't want to be spoiled completely, now would you?"

She cringed away from him on the ground. "You wouldn't...you—"

"Get up!" he snarled, the grin sliding from his face.

As she made to get to her feet he tossed the rifle behind him and slammed another roundly swinging blow to her face. She lurched backwards, falling, and before she could recover he stepped over her, planting his feet firmly, tearing the shirt from her supple body. "Thing was ready to bust anyway..."

He licked his lips again as she screamed and tried to cover herself. "Shirt sure didn't tell no lie…"

He grabbed her left wrist, twisting her arm up behind her back, forcing her to her feet.

"Sweetheart, your feeding's good—now let's see what your loving's like; the Good Lord knows you've waited a long time!"

"Don't…! Don't do it. I fed you, I…"

"More fool you, sweetheart," he rasped, cutting her off, "but you may's well get used to me; I'm going to be here quite some time. You need a man about the place."

He pushed her into the cave, noting that the candle at the rear stood beside a heavy black blanket, stretched luxuriously in a hollow on the floor.

The shadows moved in the dimness of the cave as he shoved her toward the sputtering candle. A few feet from the rear wall of rock she twisted under her own arm and pulled away from him. He laughed at the way her body moved as she tried to free herself. "No good getting all hot and bothered now, sweetheart—not with the bed all laid out for us…"

"It's not a bed!" she screamed, jerking her arm back in desperate resistance. The sweat of anticipation on his straining fingers let him down. Her hand suddenly slipped through his and he crashed backwards, off balance, onto the "bed."

There was instant, horrible movement beneath him.

"No...!" the girl screamed. "No! That's not stew, Baby, it's a man!"

But Baby, who had no ears, took no notice.

The edges of the "bed" rose up in thickly glistening, black doughy flaps—like an inky, folding pancake—and flopped purposefully over the struggling man upon it. Subtly altered digestive juices squirted into his face and muscular hardness gripped him. He gave a shriek—just one—as the living envelope around him started to squeeze.

⁂

Hours later, when the dawn was spreading like a pale stain over the horizon between the hills, the girl was still crying. Baby had taken a long time over his meal. He burped, ejecting the last bone and a few odd buttons. There wasn't even a back she could pat him on.

That day there was a new grave in the little valley in the hills. A very small one...

Somebody Calling

I'm telling my story now, after all this time, because it's not one which would have been accepted earlier without its bringing about my incarceration, and that was something I couldn't allow for reasons which will become apparent. But even as I make this statement of "confession" I feel it's worth pointing out that I don't in any way consider myself a criminal, or that the action I took those many years ago was anything other than just...and that's the other reason why I now put pen to paper: so that the police may finally close their files on a case that's lain open for far too long.

Not that this record is entirely altruistic, for in making it I also hope to salve my conscience (professionally speaking, at least) in that it was never

mine to take lives but to try to protect, extend, and preserve them. What a great shame that not all lives are worth the effort, and that there are others which should never have been brought into being in the first place.

So, here we are in the early winter of the year, certainly in the winter of my years, and in the last few hours remaining to me—my genes and my mother's nuclear legacy having finally caught up with me—it's time I told my tale....

*

A doctor, I entered the profession at the age of twenty-three; which for reasons my mother and I both understood well enough, was what she had always intended for me. And it's as well that she saw her wishes in that respect fulfilled; just a few years later she was dead from problems related to a lifetime of work at the atomic research establishment.

"Huh!" (As she had used to complain so bitterly toward the end.) "It was either that—the radiation—or those pills for depression that I'd been taking for twenty years...or perhaps both! Do you remember thalidomide, John? Remember reading about it in those medical books of yours? Well, terrible as that *stuff* was, it was no worse than aspirin compared to the poisons I was taking! If only I could prove it, but too late for that now."

And in fact too late for anything.

Somebody Calling

I missed her, of course, but life goes on—life and work, and death, eventually, and taxes always—as they are wont to have it.

Anyway, being single and of necessity solitary in my ways—even more so now that she was gone—I kept myself to myself; and despite that my workload had increased proportionally with her death, I carried on at the practice while somehow managing to cope with the additional chores at home. Life was tasteless but tenable, at least until that night a year later, when the snow lay frozen on the ground and the roads were icy black....

❦

Having driven home to where my Victorian house stands secluded at the edge of extensive woodlands, as my car's tires crunched on the gravel of the drive inside my gate, so I sensed—more than sensed, saw—that something was wrong. I get my mail at the surgery and no postman ever visits my home; what's more, I seldom have visitors of any kind, and never uninvited. So that the footprints already iced-over in my drive's thin blanket of snow might well have induced a degree of concern on their own, let alone in combination with that light in the porch, where I never left one burning!

Switching off my car's headlights and motor, I sat still, silent in the darkness. Senses alert, I listened, hearing only my own rapidly beating heart and nothing else. And the silence—the utter, unusual silence—was terrible.

Quickly I entered the house through a front door that had been forced and left standing ajar, and as quickly realized my worst fears...or perhaps not quite the worst. My study was in a state; it looked like a small whirlwind had gone through it. Several personal items—items which had sentimental value if little else—were missing. And the main living rooms were the same: all had been disarrayed, ransacked.

Upstairs, too, where in my bedroom the intruder had shown his total contempt by defecating on the Oriental carpet at the foot of my bed. Utterly appalled, again I paused to listen...and once more heard nothing. Only that same terrible silence.

Back downstairs I flew, to that place which from the first I should have investigated if I'd dared accept the concept of a worst possible scenario. And all the while I was hoping against hope that wherever else he'd been, the intruder had not discovered the small room behind the bookshelves in my library at the back of the house...but hoping in vain.

I found the door in the shelving opened up, and behind it the secret place revealed.

Inside, the light was on. The computer keyboard lay flat, apparently undisturbed on its swivel arm in front of the empty chair. The computer was working—at least it was switched on—its screen showing nothing of any importance. But other than these things and a few less important mechanical adjuncts, the room was empty, monstrously depleted.

I reeled against the wall in what little space there was, grasped my head in my trembling hands and concentrated hard on my listening. I concentrated and *concentrated*...to no avail. There was only the silence, and, beneath my straining fingers, the smooth, cold feel of the titanium plate under the skin at the back of my skull....

❦

When I had calmed down a little I considered my options, only to discover that I didn't have any! My material losses—those one or two precious personal items that had been taken—well, I could do without them. I would have to, for there was no way I could report this matter to the police. Or I could have, but that would have meant all sorts of questions, gross intrusions into my privacy, oh, and difficulties galore. Which meant that the problem was mine and mine alone, and the sooner I got down to work on it the better. But where to start?

I decided the best thing to do would be to sit still with a drink and wait for somebody to call me. For even if the call was distant and indistinct, still I might get some idea of the direction. Fortunately my drinks cabinet and its contents were intact; I poured myself a drink (as it soon would transpire, a little too much drink), and settled down to put my plan to the test...

...only to come awake with a start at 11:00 P.M., to find the remains of my drink spilled in my lap, while the house and the atmosphere were as still and as silent as ever.

Or perhaps not.

Was that a whisper I heard? Was that what had awakened me, a whisper from out there? Had somebody called?

Outside it was bitterly cold...all the better to rid my head of brandy fumes, bring my mind to bear on the job in hand. The stars glittered like ice chips in a sky where the moon was a wafer-thin crescent; the wind too was thin, cutting where it came hushing out of the woods. And yes, I thought it carried a message—a sound that went all unheard, except inside my head—the sound of somebody calling. A mayday call in fact, a cry for help, from the far side of the forest.

All very well, but if I was to make a sweep of the region beyond the woods I must first refuel my car, and I knew that at this hour the local garage wouldn't be open. Nothing for it but to wait until first light. And knowing that I wouldn't be able to sleep, still I went back into the house and tried...

*

Somebody Calling

In the still of the night somebody was calling. I remembered it the next morning when I came awake with a terrific headache. It had seemed like a dream, but my headache told me otherwise. And I certainly hadn't consumed that much brandy! But it came as no great surprise that somebody had called during the night hours; for there's nothing to get in the way at night, when everything is still and quiet.

I fueled my car, armed myself with a small scale road map of the area, and skirted the woods to their far side. And while it might have been my fevered imagination, it seemed to me that during the journey I twice heard somebody calling. On the first occasion it was the merest whisper, but on the second it was so clear that I felt sure I was closing in on the source.

A mile or two beyond the woods lay a small country village with which I was unfamiliar. External to the city's suburbs, it lay outside my area of responsibility; and, since I was more or less tied to my catchment area, by professional and personal commitments both, there had never been any need to venture this way before. Yet it was here that the second and clearest of the two calls (if, out of sheer desperation, I hadn't imagined them both) had seemed to sound so sharply on my inner ear. But as I drove along the main street toward the far end of the village, that sensation of nearness gradually receded. And I knew it was time to stop, consult my map, and get my bearings.

By then my head was aching again—as much from fear and frustration as from concentration—and for a moment or two I massaged my scalp, applying pressure to my subcutaneous plate. Then, in a while, after I had calmed down, I was able to study the map.

Obviously I had overshot the source of the calling, which had to lie somewhere between my present location and the woods farther back along my route. It couldn't be here in the actual village for the simple reason that if I had passed as close as that then of course I would have been aware immediately of its presence. It wouldn't have been that I strained to "hear" some distantly whispered SOS, rather that I would have been capable of more tangible communication…of sorts.

So, back along the way I must go, retracing my steps. But at least I knew now that the place I was looking for wasn't by the roadside but must be set well back from it.

As for my method: well, you couldn't exactly call it triangulation! More trial and error, actually. But with my map to help me, I was certainly making progress.

The map:

Two miles back, midway between the village and the woods, I had noticed a crossroads. It was there on the map: an unmetalled road, more properly a track, crossing at right angles the road down which I had driven. In both directions, east and west of the main road, several properties stood well back in marked isolation. I suspected they'd be neglected farm buildings; the land here and the people who worked it were not much known for their productivity.

And so I drove back to the crossroads, pulled to the side of the road, and sat there with my window rolled down, cool in a wintry breeze. And I concentrated, concentrated, until—

—There!

Somebody was calling! I felt my head almost inadvertently turning to the east, and then knew for certain that my way lay in that direction, that somebody was there.

And now my fear had turned to anger, and my anger in turn was building and my scalp tingling as I drove slowly along the track toward a clump of near-distant, dilapidated buildings. I could actually feel somebody drawing closer moment by moment—yet nevertheless gave a start when suddenly I "heard:"

John! I feel you now. I feel you near. Come for me, John. Come quickly!

⁂

There was a paddock behind a leaning gate, stables with sagging roofs, and a farmhouse with several boarded windows—but smoke wafted from a chimney in the end wall, and a battered white van stood in what was once the farmyard. I drove off the track into the cover of a copse and went the rest of the way on foot. And:

John! somebody called again, clear as spoken words now. *He has a weapon!* And the picture of a shotgun formed in my mind.

I paused behind a lean-to full of rusting farm implements. *Is he with you now?*

No, I think he must be sleeping. He was...he was sort of busy last night.

Busy? The short hairs at the back of my neck prickled, but I just had to ask, *How, busy?*

He was...he was doing things...three times, but I'm not hurt.

I glanced at my watch. It was 8:45, still quite early, and if he'd been (I couldn't help but shudder) "doing things" last night, then it seemed highly likely that somebody was right and he'd be sleeping it off.

I edged up to the door of the house, put my ear to the old oak panels and listened. Silence. Good. The door was locked but just a few paces away a sash window lifted at my touch, its dry pulleys squealing a very little. Heart pounding, I was over the sill in a moment, the sash falling shut behind me but this time silently. And brushing aside the rags of moth-eaten curtains, I paused again to listen...and was thankful to hear nothing.

In the sickly yellowish light from the grimy, fly-specked window, I looked round the room. It didn't appear to be in use. A few sticks of furniture were thick with dust and cobwebs, and the old, mold-stained wallpaper was peeling in several places.

The air was tainted, stagnant. A door on my left led to a corridor, the main passage into the house from the front door. And somewhere in or just beyond the passage, a dim red glow pulsed on and off with mechanical regularity in the gloom.

My first thought was that perhaps the house was alarmed—that in opening the window I might have initiated some sort of security system—but if that were so, then why had the house continued to remain as quiet as a tomb?

Crossing carefully to the door, I looked into the passage and saw a second room on the other side. Its door was standing open, with an area of its interior visible, so that I was able to make out the source of the pulsing light—a computer console, with a screen that was blank except for a small red light whose steady winking indicated the computer's standby mode.

Breathing just a little easier, I slid across the corridor and into the room of the computer...and saw at once that this place was very much the center of the house. It was tidy if not too clean, with one wall that was shelved floor to ceiling, and another that had been whitewashed over to serve as a screen for the combined video/CD projector that was situated near the computer console. The wall shelving was full of labeled cassettes and discs, but right then I wasn't able to study the subject of this considerable collection.

I did, however, pick up and break open the double-barreled shotgun which I found standing in one corner near the door. The gun was loaded; easing it shut again, I balanced its comforting weight in the crook of my arm. As might be imagined, from then on I felt a lot more secure as I continued to explore the rest of the house.

Downstairs there wasn't very much more to see: a kitchen, toilet, and small living room, where the last few embers of an open fire glowed in a grimy grate. But as well as the doors to these rooms there was another, far stouter door in the passage...and it was locked. All of the rooms were in a filthy state and I didn't linger in any of them, but as for the locked door in the passage—that was where I was most aware of somebody's proximity, and knew that somebody must be aware of mine. Knowing what I was about, however, she made no comment that might startle or disturb me.

She, yes.

Forgive me. This was the only way I could do it: by telling the story my way, by building to where I've left myself no choice but to reveal everything—this secret I've kept these many years—which even now I'm loath to divulge. But give me a moment...I need a moment to compose myself, also to compose the rest of this, and then I'll get done....

Somebody Calling

I found him upstairs in one of the bedrooms.

Having heard me climbing the creaking stairs, he was out of bed, stumbling around the room and trying to dress himself. I saw stained, dirty underclothes, a gross, hairy body, a fat red face full of stubble set with a large, loose-lipped mouth and little piggy eyes that glared their hatred and fear. And: "What?" he grunted, fastening his belt buckle. "Who?" as he reached for a stained shirt draped across a bedside table.

"Don't bother," I told him, aiming the shotgun. "You can forget the shirt, the vest will do. Downstairs, and don't try anything silly. I'm not a very good shot, but with this thing I don't need to be."

"My shoes," he grunted, reaching for them where they lay on the floor beside his bed.

"No shoes." I shook my head. They were something he might try to throw at me.

And now he began to bluster. "Who the fuck are you? What do you think you're doing, breaking into my house like this?"

"I'm arresting you," I answered.

"Arresting me? For what? In civilian clothing…you're no policeman." Now that he was awake, he was beginning to look a lot more dangerous.

"I'm Detective Inspector John McKenzie," I lied. "I don't wear a uniform. Now get downstairs, and quickly. There are one or two things we have to talk about."

Squat and waddling, breathing heavily and muttering under his breath, he started down the stairs, pausing just once until I was obliged to prod him in the back of the neck with the twin barrels of his gun. And in the living room I sat him in a chair before moving over to a set of drawers.

Rummaging in the top drawer I found what I wanted: a roll of adhesive tape. And before he could give it too much thought I moved around behind him. But the way his eyes swiveled this way and that, like a trapped lizard's, I could see what he was thinking: that I would have to put the shotgun down in order to tie him up...and he probably wondered why I was bothering to restrain him in the first place.

So I did put the gun down—I put its butt down, hard, on the crown of his head. Then, while he lolled to and fro, half-stunned, I taped his thick wrists to the chair's arms, his fat neck to its headrest, and his dirty feet to its legs. And when he looked like he could speak again, I said:

"She's in the cellar, isn't she?"

"She?" he mumbled in return. "I don't know any she."

"Well, then," I said, "somebody is in the cellar, right?"

To which he answered, "Fuck off and die!"

I put the barrels of the gun against his ear and said, "If you don't tell me where the key is, I'm going to kill you. This gun—both barrels—should take your head right off those ugly sloping shoulders of yours."

"Huh…huh…who the fuck are you?" His voice was only a whisper now, or more properly a thin croak.

"I'm her brother," I told him. "Her twin brother."

And it was true—it *is* true—that I'm somebody's twin brother, her Siamese twin.

We were born back-to-back, joined at the back of our heads, even sharing a little brain stuff. We both had our own brains, but there was joining stuff, too. When they separated us, they said I stood a chance but somebody would probably die. I think they wanted her to die, but our mother didn't. Mother was one of those pro-lifers, also an untouchable. She'd never been to prenatal, never been examined, never been X-rayed or anything of that nature. But even if she had been it wouldn't have made even the slightest difference; she was pregnant, determined to deliver, and even more determined to care for her child…in fact, her children.

So she'd taken us home—both of us—and cared for us, and somebody hadn't died.

When we were five we had our plates fitted (mother paid a specialist for somebody's plate; she paid for his silence, too, because by then my twin was supposed to have died), and I got a new one when I was seventeen. Somebody hadn't needed a new one because her skull was already full-grown when she was five, or at least it was as big as it would get.

But let me go back a little. So they'd separated us, yes, but not entirely. What I mean is, some kind of tenuous connection remained. Tenuous at a distance but much stronger when we were close. Telepathy? Well, I know it sounds like it, but no, not exactly. It was awareness rather than knowing, and feeling rather than hearing. And yes, it was loving, too. I mean, how can you fail to love someone who you know loves—relies upon, depends upon, would *really* die without— you? And after all, I was only doing what our mother had wanted me to do: being a doctor, then a carer, someone to tend to somebody's needs, if or when she was sick.

As for her name:

She'd never had a proper name, was never christened. And when we'd tried to give her one, my mother and I, she wouldn't accept it. Even as a child, an infant, she'd known that people had names. And somebody had never considered herself a person. But then, apart from her mother and brother, nor would anyone else consider her a person—ever.

She had thought of herself as nobody, and it had been up to mother and me to convince her that she was somebody, which finally she'd accepted. She'd allowed herself to be somebody, with a small "s" that loaned her the anonymity she craved.

And now somebody was downstairs, in the cellar…

※

The key was on a narrow dusty ledge above the door frame. But as I unlocked the door somebody said, if not in so many words, *John, I'm very cold*. It was more that I myself gave an involuntary shiver as I felt her mind touch mine. And then finally I went down to where somebody lay in a cobwebbed corner under a dirty sheet on an old stained mattress.

I wrapped her in my coat, bundled her upstairs and along the passage, kicked open the front door and went to my car. I put her on the front passenger seat, turned on the engine and the heater, and asked her, "Will you be all right? Just for a minute or two."

Yes, John, she answered, and made familiar sucking sounds with the blowhole-cum-feeding orifice in the side of her face. *I'll be okay now. Please be careful.*

With only one thought, one intention in mind, I went back into the house. But I'm not a killer by nature—anything but—and first I had to know something more about my burglar. The answer I sought might be there in the room of the computer and projector. And for the next fifteen minutes I played discs and tapes of the utmost depravity onto the whitewashed wall screen.

Men with dwarves, with other men and amputees, with grotesquely obese women and emaciated, almost skeletal girls; also with animals—pigs, dogs, sheep, and ponies. Bound women with running sores, scar-tissue for breasts, and shaven lice-ridden heads; one such lying on her back, drinking the urine of three men through a tin funnel.

As for the loathsome being I'd left tied to a chair, well he featured in far too many of these…these what? Entertainments? They went on and on, seemingly vying with each other to be the most repulsive, each of them worse than the last. Twice I threw up before shutting everything down and returning to my captive….

*

He was struggling like a madman to free himself from the chair, rocking from side to side, forward and back. And when he saw me come into the room he redoubled his efforts.

"Do you want me to hit you again?" I asked him.

"Fuck you!" he gasped. "You and that fucking thing."

"She's my sister," I said, "my twin, and you must be made to pay for what you've done."

"I didn't mean to…to take her," he panted, exhausted from his struggles. "I was after money, jewelry—anything I could sell for a few quid."

"But you did take her," I answered. "And what's more, you *have* taken her!"

"You don't know anything!" He blustered.

"I know everything," I told him.

"I'm no worse than you!" He yelled hoarsely. "Her brother? Well, that's as may be, but nobody would keep a thing like that if he wasn't fucking it!"

I almost threw up again, then put the shotgun to his head and said, "You…are a very sick man. But you're right about one thing: I'm not a policeman, I'm a doctor. And I think that maybe I can help you."

He saw what he thought was a ray of hope, decided to play it for all it was worth, licked his lips and blinked his piggy eyes at me. And then he said, "Do you…do you think you can cure me?"

"Oh, I'm really quite sure of it," I said, squeezing both triggers and recoiling a little from the blast…

*

After that—

—I tossed some sticks of furniture into the sitting room, tore down moldering curtains to drape haphazardly through all the downstairs

rooms, and laid a trail of torn newspapers from the hot embers in the grate to the curtains, the furniture and all. Then I waited until I saw the first flames come creeping, and with that it was done.

It was snowing fairly heavily by the time I'd reached the main road, but back there in the near-distance the dense black smoke was already rising to the sky....

Later, back home with somebody, I washed and fed her, examined her for bruises and...and whatever. But apart from her obvious weariness she seemed no worse for wear. So I let her sleep the morning out in her cot, and before I went off late to work returned her to the small room behind the bookshelves.

And that's where I left her, as always, in the cushioned chair from which she could reach her long feeding straw on the left—reach it with the hole in her face—and the computer's swiveling keyboard on the right, with the three-fingered hand on her only limb, a solitary elbow.

For that was where somebody felt happiest, or at least as happy as she ever felt: in control of her own little window on a world she would never see or visit except like this, through the plain oblong shape of her computer screen. There again, at least the screen had a recognizable shape...

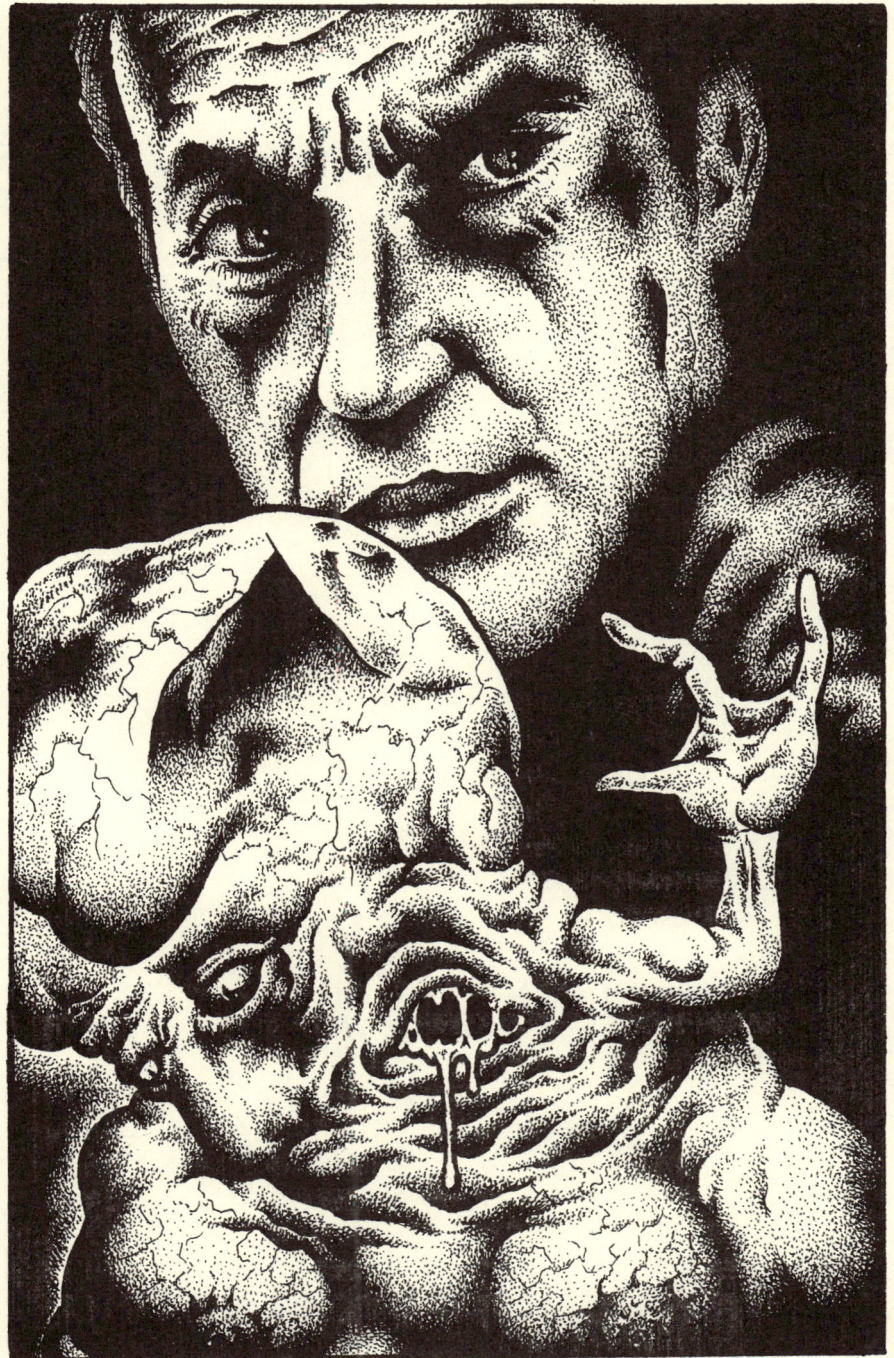

It was all a long time ago, but now it's over. My genes and/or mother's nuclear legacy have caught up with me, caught up with somebody, too, and it's time to end it all. No big deal—just Big "C"—and in a way we welcome the end, somebody and me.

We'll fade away together, in touch as always, as sweet as I can make it with a sharp needle and the very gentlest drugs. And if I believed in God, why I might even look forward to it, much as somebody does. Oh yes, for my sister is convinced that however we look in life, our souls are ravishingly beautiful.

But more than that, she also believes that after her soul is set free, finally she'll be Somebody....